Monstrosities

Monstrosities

CHARLES FUGE

RED FOX

A Red Fox Book
Published by Random Century Children's Books
20 Vauxhall Bridge Road, London SW1V 2SA

An imprint of the Random Century Group
London   Melbourne   Sydney   Auckland
Johannesburg and agencies throughout the world

First published by Hutchinson Children's Books 1989
Red Fox edition 1991

Set in 13/15 pt Sabon by Deltatype Ltd, Ellesmere Port
Printed and bound in Great Britain by
Scotprint, Musselburgh, Scotland

ISBN 0 09 967330 4

The Ogglewop

The Ogglewop is tall and wide,
And though he looks quite passive,
He's crammed with boys and girls inside,
– That's why he is so massive!

Colin West

1

The Wendigo

The Wendigo,
The Wendigo!
Its eyes are ice and indigo!
Its blood is rank and yellowish!
Its voice is hoarse and bellowish!
Its tentacles are slithery,
And scummy,
Slimy,
Leathery!
Its lips are hungry blubbery,
And smacky,
Sucky,
Rubbery!
The Wendigo,
The Wendigo!
I saw it just a friend ago!
Last night it lurked in Canada;
Tonight, on your veranada!
As you are lolling hammockwise,
It contemplates you stomachwise.
You loll,
It contemplates,
It lollops.
The rest is merely gulps and gollops.

Ogden Nash

the fungus fingers

where the icebergs break in splinters
where the glaciers melt and flow
where the snow is deep as houses
   there the fungus fingers go

where the lightning rips the sky cloth
where the sunburst blinds your eye
where the rain dissolves high mountains
   there the fungs fingers fly

where the islands drown in oceans
where the monsters growl and call
where the forests shake with anger
   there the fungus fingers crawl

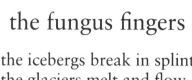

where the Space Police are wide-eyed
where the skulls dry in the sun
where the laser beams split planets
   there the fungus fingers run

where the echoes boom through valleys
where the ghostly shadows creep
where the night falls like a hammer
   there
   the
   fungus
   fingers
   LEAP!

Wes Magee

The Malfeasance

It was a dark, dank, dreadful night
And while millions were abed
The Malfeasance bestirred itself
And raised its ugly head.

The leaves dropped quietly in the night,
In the sky Orion shone;
The Malfeasance bestirred itself
Then crawled around till dawn.

Taller than a chimney stack,
More massive than a church,
It slithered to the city
With a purpose and a lurch.

Squelch, squelch, the scaly feet
Flapped along the roads;
Nothing like it had been seen
Since a recent fall of toads.

Bullets bounced off the beast,
Aircraft made it grin;
Its open mouth made an eerie sound
Uglier than sin.

Still it floundered forwards,
Still the city reeled;
There was panic on the pavements,
Even policemen squealed.

Then suddenly someone suggested
(As the beast had done no harm)
It would be kinder to show it kindness,
Better to stop the alarm.

When they offered it refreshment
The creature stopped in its track;
When they waved a greeting to it
Steam rose from its back.

As its friendliness grew firmer
The problem was quietly solved;
Terror turned to triumph and
The Malfeasance dissolved.

And where it stood there hung a mist,
And in its wake a shining trail,
And the people found each other
And thereby hangs a tale.

Alan Bold

The spangled
pandemonium

The spangled pandemonium
Is missing from the zoo.
He bent the bars the barest bit,
And slithered glibly through.

He crawled across the moated wall,
He climbed the mango tree,
And when the keeper scrambled up,
He nipped him in the knee.

To all of you, a warning
Not to wander after dark,
Or if you must, make very sure
You stay out of the park.

For the spangled pandemonium
Is missing from the zoo,
And since he nipped his keeper,
He would just as soon nip you.

Palmer Brown

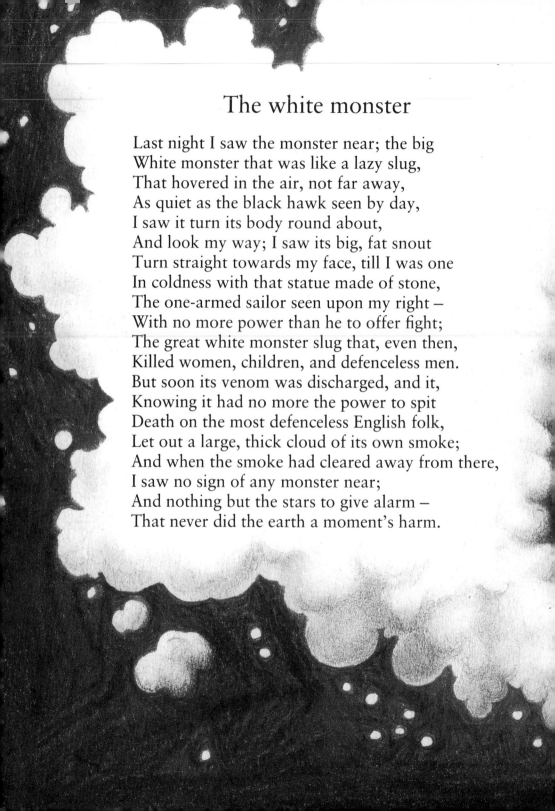

The white monster

Last night I saw the monster near; the big
White monster that was like a lazy slug,
That hovered in the air, not far away,
As quiet as the black hawk seen by day,
I saw it turn its body round about,
And look my way; I saw its big, fat snout
Turn straight towards my face, till I was one
In coldness with that statue made of stone,
The one-armed sailor seen upon my right –
With no more power than he to offer fight;
The great white monster slug that, even then,
Killed women, children, and defenceless men.
But soon its venom was discharged, and it,
Knowing it had no more the power to spit
Death on the most defenceless English folk,
Let out a large, thick cloud of its own smoke;
And when the smoke had cleared away from there,
I saw no sign of any monster near;
And nothing but the stars to give alarm –
That never did the earth a moment's harm.

Oh, it was strange to see a thing like jelly,
An ugly, boneless thing all back and belly,
Among the peaceful stars – that should have been
A mile deep in the sea, and never seen:
A big, fat, lazy slug that, even then,
Killed women, children, and defenceless men.

W. H. Davies

Little boy lost

The wood was rather old and dark
The witch was very ugly
And if it hadn't been for father
Walking there so smugly
I never should have followed
The beckoning of her finger.
Ah me how long ago it was
And still I linger
Under the ever interlacing beeches
Over a carpet of moss
I lift my hand but it never reaches
To where the breezes toss
The sun-kissed leaves above.
The sun?
Beware.
The sun never comes here.
Round about and round I go
Up and down and to and fro
The woodlouse hops upon the tree
Or should do but I really cannot see.
Happy fellow. Why can't I be
Happy as he?
The wood grows darker every day
It's not a bad place in a way
But I lost the way
Last Tuesday
Did I love father, mother, home?

Not very much; but now they're gone
I think of them with kindly toleration
Bred inevitably of separation.
Really if I could find some food
I should be happy enough in this wood
But darker days and hungrier I must spend
Till hunger and darkness make an end.

Stevie Smith

A small dragon

I've found a small dragon in the woodshed.
Think it must have come from deep inside a forest
because it's damp and green and leaves
are still reflecting in its eyes.

I fed it on many things, tried grass,
the roots of stars, hazelnut and dandelion,
but it stared up at me as if to say, I need
food you can't provide.

It made a nest among the coal,
not unlike a bird's but larger,
it's out of place here
and is quite silent.

If you believed in it I would come
hurrying to your house to let you share my wonder,
but I want instead to see
if you yourself will pass this way.

Brian Patten

Prince Kano

In a dark wood Prince Kano lost his way
And searched in vain through the long summer's day.
At last, when night was near, he came in sight
Of a small clearing filled with yellow light,
And there, bending beside his brazier, stood
A charcoal burner wearing a black hood.
The Prince cried out for joy: 'Good friend, I'll give
What you will ask: guide me to where I live.'
The man pulled back his hood: he had no face –
Where it should be there was an empty space.

Half dead with fear the Prince staggered away,
Rushed blindly through the wood till break of day;
And then he saw a larger clearing, filled
With houses, people, but his soul was chilled;
He looked around for comfort, and his search
Led him inside a small, half-empty church
Where monks prayed. 'Father,' to one he said,
'I've seen a dreadful thing; I am afraid.'
'What did you see, my son?' 'I saw a man
Whose face was like . . .' and, as the Prince began,
The monk drew back his hood and seemed to hiss,
Pointing to where his face should be, 'Like this?'

Edward Lowbury

15

The Snitterjipe

In mellowy orchards, rich and ripe,
Is found the luminous Snitterjipe.
Bad boys who climb the bulging trees
Feel his sharp breath about their knees;
His trembling whiskers tickle so,
They squeak and squeal till they let go.

They hear his far-from-friendly bark;
They see his eyeballs in the dark
Shining and shifting in their sockets
As round and big as pears in pockets
They feel his hot and wrinkly hide;
They see his nostrils flaming wide,
His tapering teeth, his jutting jaws,
His tongue, his tail, his twenty claws
His hairy shadow in the moon
It makes them sweat, it makes them
    swoon;
And as they climb the orchard wall,
They let their pilfered pippins fall.
The Snitterjipe suspends pursuit
And falls upon the fallen fruit;
And while they flee the monster fierce,
Apples, not boys, his talons pierce.
With thumping hearts they hear him munch –
Six apples at a time he'll crunch.
At length he falls asleep, and they
On tiptoe take their homeward way.
But long before the blackbirds pipe
To welcome day, the Snitterjipe
Has fled afar, and on the green
Only his fearsome prints are seen.

James Reeves

The ghoul

The gruesome ghoul, the grisly ghoul,
without the slightest noise
waits patiently beside the school
to feast on girls and boys.

He lunges fiercely through the air
as they come out to play,
then grabs a couple by the hair
and drags them far away.

He cracks their bones and snaps their
    backs
and squeezes out their lungs;
he chews their thumbs like candy snacks
and pulls apart their tongues.

He slices their stomachs and bites their
    hearts
and tears their flesh to shreds;
he swallows their toes like toasted tarts
and gobbles down their heads.

Fingers, elbows, hands and knees
and arms and legs and feet –
he eats them with delight and ease,
for every part's a treat.

And when the gruesome, grisly ghoul
has nothing left to chew,
he hurries to another school
and waits . . . perhaps for you.

Jack Prelutsky

Green man in the garden

Green man in the garden
  Staring from the tree,
Why do you look so long and hard
  Through the pane at me?

Your eyes are dark as holly,
    Of sycamore your horns,
Your bones are made of elder-branch,
    Your teeth are made of thorns.

Your hat is made of ivy-leaf,
    Of bark your dancing shoes,
And evergreen and green and green
    Your jacket and shirt and trews.

Leave your house and leave your land
    And throw away the key,
And never look behind, he creaked,
    And come and live with me.

I bolted up the window,
    I bolted up the door,
I drew the blind that I should find
    The green man never more.

But when I softly turned the stair
    As I went up to bed,
I saw the green man standing there.
    Sleep well, my friend, he said.

                                    Charles Causley

The Sloojee

The Sloojee strikes on nights like this,
When everything is still,
It strikes you if you snore too much,
And makes you feel quite ill.

It makes you cry, it makes you weep,
It makes you mutter in your sleep,
It makes you frown, it makes you fidget,
It makes you wish you were a midget.

It makes you wince, it makes you twice,
It makes your kneecaps turn to ice,
It makes you moan, it makes you wail,
It makes you chew your fingernails.

It makes you scream, it makes you shriek,
It makes you itchy for a week,
It makes you shake, it makes you shiver,
It makes you grateful for your liver.

It makes you spit, it makes you shout,
It makes your teeth and hair fall out,
It makes you twitch, it makes you tremble,
It makes your hip joint reassemble.

The Sloojee strikes, and having struck,
The Sloojee slobbers on,
For when you cease to snore out loud,
It knows its job is done.

Colin West

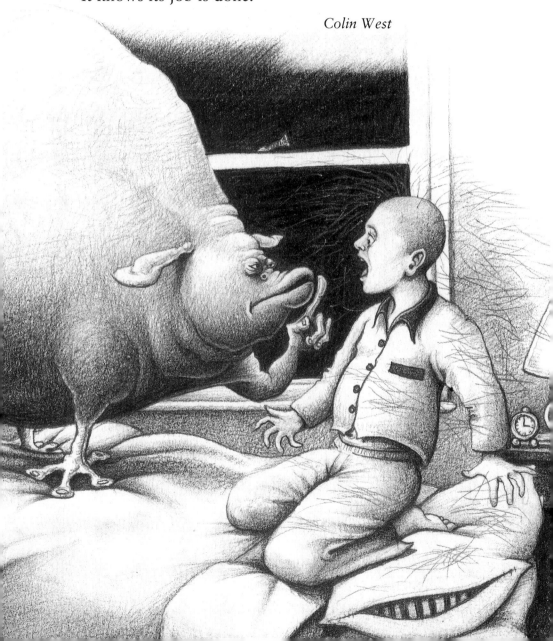

Infant Song

Don't you love my baby, mam,
Lying in his little pram,

Polished all with water clean,
The finest baby ever seen?

Daughter, daughter, if I could
I'd love your baby as I should,

But why the suit of signal red,
The horns that grow out of his head,

Why does he burn with brimstone heat,
Have cloven hooves instead of feet,

Fishing hooks upon each hand,
The keenest tail that's in the land,

Pointed ears and teeth so stark
And eyes that flicker in the dark?

Don't you love my baby, mam?

Dearest, I do not think I can.
I do not, do not think I can.

Charles Causley

24

Nightmare

I never say his name aloud
and don't tell anybody
I always close all the drawers
and look behind the door before I go to bed
I cross my toes and count to eight
and turn the pillow over three times
Still he comes sometimes
one two three
like a shot
glaring at me with his eyes,
grating with his nails
and sneering his big sneer –
the Scratch Man

Oh-oh, now I said his name!
Mama, I can't sleep!

Siv Widerberg

The Mewlips

The shadows where the Mewlips dwell
Are dark and wet as ink,
And slow and softly rings their bell,
As in the slime you sink.

You sink into the slime, who dare
To knock upon their door,
While down the grinning gargoyles stare
And noisome waters pour.

Beside the rotting river-strand
The drooping willows weep,
And gloomily the gorcrows stand
Croaking in their sleep.

Over the Merlock Mountains a long and weary way,
In a mouldy valley where the trees are grey,
By a dark pool's borders without wind or tide,
Moonless and sunless, the Mewlips hide.

The cellars where the Mewlips sit
Are deep and dank and cold
With single sickly candle lit;
And there they count their gold.

Their walls are wet, their ceilings drip,
　　Their feet upon the floor
Go softly with a squish-flap-flip,
　　As they sidle to the door.

They peep out slyly; through a crack
　　Their feeling fingers creep,
And when they've finished, in a sack
　　Your bones they take to keep.

Beyond the Merlock Moutains, a long and lonely road,
Through the spider-shadows and the marsh of Tode,
And through the wood of hanging trees and the
　　　　gallows-weed,
You go to find the Mewlips – and the Mewlips feed.

J. R. R. Tolkien

The old false leg

Three crows hopped on an old false leg,
   On an old false leg,
   An old false leg,
Three crows hopped on an old false leg
   Which lay out alone on the moor.

Whoever could have dropped that old false leg,
   Old false leg,
   That old false leg,
Whoever could have dropped that old false leg
   Out by the lake on the moor?

It was nobody dropped that old false leg,
   Old false leg,
   Old false leg,
It was nobody dropped that very false leg,
   Which slept out alone on the moor.

That old false leg jumped up on its toes,
   Up on its toes,
   Up on its toes,
That old false leg jumped up on its toes,
   In the very wet mist on the moor.

And it hit the tail feathers off those crows,
   Off those crows,
   Off those crows,
And it hit the tail feathers off those crows,
   Caw, caw, caw on the moor.

And those crows flew away quite nakedly,
   Quite nakedly,
   Quite nakedly,
And those crows flew away quite nakedly,
   Into the mist on the moor.

And the false leg thereupon strolled to the shore,
   Strolled to the shore,
   Strolled to the shore,
And the false leg leg thereupon strolled to the
   shore,
   Into the lake, and was seen no more.

Geoffrey Grigson

29

Welsh incident

'But that was nothing to what things came out
From the sea-caves of Criccieth yonder.'
'What were they? Mermaids? dragons? ghosts?'
'Nothing at all of any things like that.'
'What were they, then?'
                        'All sorts of queer things,
Things never seen or heard or written about,
Very strange, un-Welsh, utterly peculiar
Things. Oh, solid enough they seemed to touch,
Had anyone dared it. Marvellous creations,
All various shapes and sizes, and no sizes,
All new, each perfectly unlike his neighbour.
Though all came moving slowly out together.
'Describe just one of them.'
                        'I am unable.'
'What were their colours?'
                        'Mostly nameless colours.
Colours you'd like to see; but one was puce
Or perhaps more like crimson, but not purplish
Some had no colour.'
                        'Tell me, had they legs?'
'Not a leg nor foot among them that I saw.'
'But did these things come out in any order?
What o'clock was it? What was the day of the week?
Who else was present? How was the weather?'
'I was coming to that. It was half-past three
On Easter Tuesday last. The sun was shining.

The Harlech Silver Band played *Marchog Jesu*
On thirty-seven shimmering instruments,
Collecting for Caernarvon's (Fever) Hospital Fund.
The populations of Pwllheli, Criccieth,
Portmadoc, Borth, Tremadoc, Penrhyndeudraeth,
Were all assembled. Criccieth's mayor addressed them
First in good Welsh and then in fluent English.
Twisting his fingers in his chain of office,
Welcoming the things. They came out on the sand,
Not keeping time to the band, moving seaward
Silently at a snail's pace. But at last
The most odd, indescribable thing of all,
Which hardly one man there could see for wonder,
Did something recognizably a something.'
'Well, what?'
                    'It made a noise.'
                                   'A frightening noise?'
'No, no.'
            'A musical noise? A noise of scuffling?'
'No, but a very loud, respectable noise –
Like groaning to oneself on Sunday morning
In Chapel, close before the second psalm.'
'What did the mayor do?'
                              'I was coming to that.'

Robert Graves

Dragon poem

He comes in the night, killing all greenery,
with his spiky tail and rough scabby skin
killing all the humans and spitting the bones
   in the bin.

Frances Edwards (aged 11)

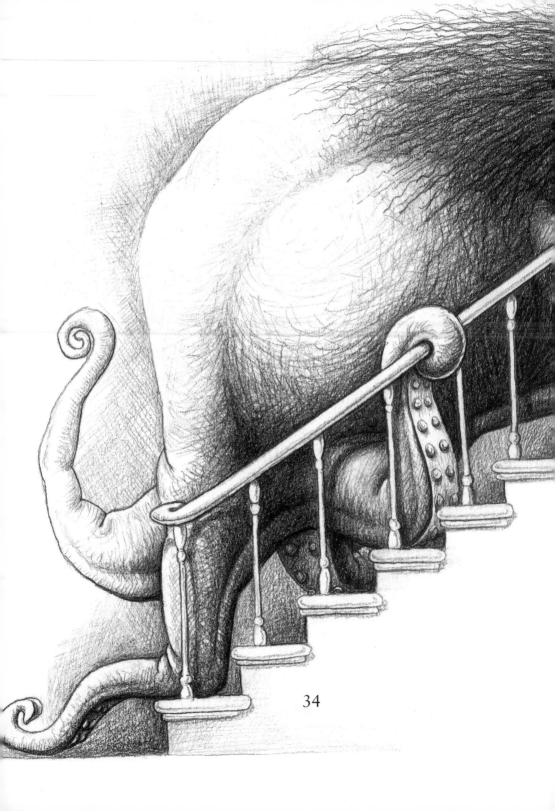

34

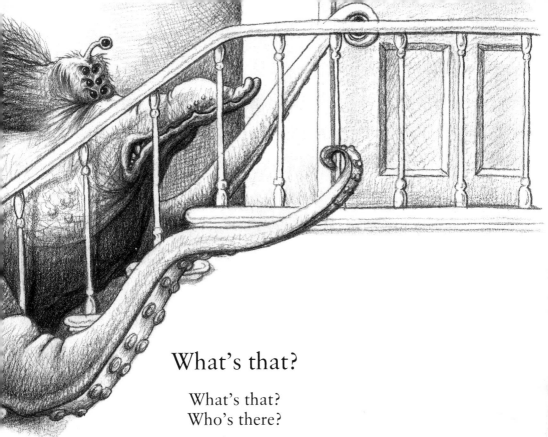

What's that?

What's that?
Who's there?

There's a great huge horrible HORRIBLE
creeping up the stair!
A huge big terrible TERRIBLE
with creepy crawly hair!
There's a ghastly grisly GHASTLY
with seven slimy eyes!
And flabby grabby tentacles
of a gigantic size!
He's crept into my room now,
he's leaning over me.
I wonder if he's thinking
How delicious I will be.

Florence Parry Heide

On the island of strange mutations

There were six heads,
Identical sextuplets.
The first head wore no make-up, child of nature.
The second head made itself up to the eyes.
The third head was a brunette.
The fourth head tried tints, ash-blonde and auburn.
The fifth head wore a bright smile.
The sixth head had downcast lips.
The first head said, I am tired, I must rest.
The second head said, I am wide awake, I want to dance.
The third head said, Have you a cigarette?
The fourth head said, Lung cancer, I am giving up.
The fifth head said, Never leave me.
The sixth head said, I can't bear being tied down.
Six heads
On a single body, the body of Scylla;
Lovely wrangling heads.
They were forced to yield to each other
Like traffic at an experimental roundabout.
When some felt merely alone, others felt lonely.
When some were stuffing, others were on a diet.
Some wanted a career, others wanted domesticity.
They agreed on one thing only:
Life was all complication and pain,
They longed for harmony and simplicity.

Yet whenever they mentioned this,
The fact that they were in agreement
Produced a terrible boredom and ennui
In Scylla: she had to quarrel with herself again.

D. M. Thomas

The moonwuzo's sea-song

Who is that walking on the dark sea sand?
The old Bride of the Wind

What is that staring out of the weedy pool?
The newborn Monster in its caul

What is that eerie chanting from the foam?
The mermaid's gardening song

What is that shadow floating on the water?
The Fish-King's daughter

Who bears those candles down by the Sea's curled rim?
The children going home

Cara Lockhart Smith

caul: membrane which sometimes covers a child's head when it is
born — once believed to be a lucky charm against drowning

I am Boj

I am Boj
I crackle like the Wig of a Judge

I am Boj
My eyes boil over with Hodge-Podge

I am Boj
Organized Sludge and a Thunder-Wedge

I am Boj
I am a Tower of Solid Grudge

I am Boj
The molten Centre, the cutting Edge

I am Boj
from blackest Dudgeon I swing my Bludgeon

I am Boj.

Adrian Mitchell

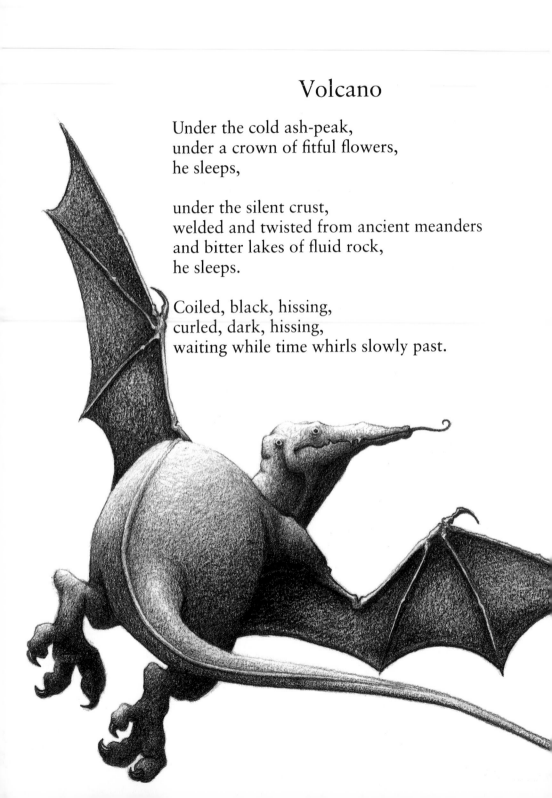

Volcano

Under the cold ash-peak,
under a crown of fitful flowers,
he sleeps,

under the silent crust,
welded and twisted from ancient meanders
and bitter lakes of fluid rock,
he sleeps.

Coiled, black, hissing,
curled, dark, hissing,
waiting while time whirls slowly past.

(A thousand years
in the blink of a slow stone eye.)

Rain washes his back,
smoothing mud into the crevices,
helping grass to dress him in summer clothing.

Trees clutch him with fingered roots,
But never deep enough to spoil his sleep,
Never deep enough to ruffle his hot dreams.

But once upon a time, just as a soft summer
is folding itself into autumn,
his hiss becomes a roar,
His skin cracks and stretches,
His black jaws open in a vast and fiery yawn.

The surprised grass crackles and blackens,
and floats away;
Trees wave like torches and dissolve;
His skin heaves and splits,
folds and breaks
as the snake swiftly rises,
and tumbles and rumbles
into the broken and burning valley.

Up into the sky
on wings that cover the sun,
the black dragon flies.

41　　　　　*Christopher Mann*

Monster

I saw a monster in the woods
As I was cycling by,
His footsteps smouldered in the leaves,
His breath made bushes die,

And when he raised his hairy arm
It blotted out the sun;
He snatched a pigeon from the sky
And swallowed it in one.

His mouth was like a dripping cave,
His eyes like pools of lead,
And when he growled I rode back home
And rushed upstairs to bed.

But that was yesterday and though
It gave me quite a fright,
I'm older now and braver so
I'm going back tonight.

I'll tie him up when he's asleep
And take him to the zoo.
The trouble is he's rather big . . .
Will you come too?

Richard Edwards

The boodlespook

It's the boodlespook you nincompoop
Of course it's not a dwarf
He's really more than two foot four
But you see he has a stoop
And so would you with three left feet
Two size ten and one size eight
And a pair of arms too short to meet
It's the boodlespook you creep.
It's the boodlespook you utter clot
How can you say you think it's not
What else do you know that's only got
Eleven teeth, with nine on top
And two beneath, but the boodlespook?
It's the boodlespook you barnacle
Of course he wears a monocle
And so would you with just one eye
And that one pointing at the sky
It's the boodlespook you silly chump
It's nothing like a heffalump.
Does a heffalump have turquoise toes
Or a daffodil where its nose should grow
And do heffalumps talk spookabuzz?
Of course they don't, but the boodle does.

It's the boodlespook you drippy wet
I've told you now so don't forget
And if you see him walking by
Don't point or stare or give a cry
Or laugh at him – he's not a fluke
Remember now, he's the boodlespook.

Anon.

The wolf spider

Lurking among the grass-root knots
pounces a creature, merciless, cunning –
A spider with eight enormous hairy legs – oh –
It's as big as a wolf and it's running,
   running, running.

Not a web-spinner
which lies in wait for its dinner
Of flies which blunder and buzz
but a wolf spider
who runs down his prey
As the lone timber wolf does.

               R. C. Scriven

Screaming

I hate the sound of screaming –
When horrors pull your hair,
When shutters bang and doorbells clang
But nobody is there.

When yellow eyes are gleaming,
But they are all you see,
I hate the sound of screaming –
Especially when it's me!

Doug MacLeod

The earth-ling

Countless years ago the people of Alzorus used the planet Earth as a lunatic asylum. They called the people they dumped there 'earth-lings'.

I am an earth-ling.
My memory goes back a long way.
I was dumped here long ago.
I lived beneath some overhanging rocks.
Around me at night, through the sky's black sheet,
stars poured down.
It was lonely sitting for centuries
beneath that rain-drenched rock,
wrapped in furs, afraid of this whole terrible planet.
I grew fed up with the taste of its food.
I made fire, I slaughtered creatures,
I walked through a forest and made friends.
I copied the things they made.
I walked through another forest and found enemies,
I destroyed the things they made.
I went on and on and on and on,
and on a bit more.
I crossed mountains, I crossed new oceans.
I became familiar with this world.
Time would not stop running when I asked it.
I could not whistle for it to come back.
I invented a couple of languages.
I wrote things down.
I invented books.

Time passed.

My inventions piled up. The natives of this planet
feared me.

Some tried to destroy me.

Rats came. A great plague swept over the world.

Many of me died.

I am an earth-ling.

I invented cities. I tore them down.

I sat in comfort. I sat in poverty. I sat in boredom.

Home was a planet called Alzorus. A tiny far off star —
One night it went out. It vanished.
I am an earth-ling, exiled for ever from my beginnings.
Time passed. I did things. Time passed. I grew exhausted.
One day
A great fire swept the world.
I wanted to go back to the beginning.
It was impossible.
The rock I had squatted under melted.
Friends became dust,
Dust became the only friend.
In the dust I drew faces of people.
I am putting this message on a feather
and puffing it up among the stars.
I have missed so many things out!
But this is the basic story, the terrible story.
I am an earth-ling,
I was dumped here long ago.
Mistakes were made.

Brian Patten

The horny-goloch

The horny-goloch is an awesome beast,
Soople an scaly;
It has twa horns, an a hantle o feet,
An a forkie tailie.

Anon.

Gloshery

Over the mud-marish, glimbles were glowing,
And home-tramping, slowish, momyls were lowing,
And, as the glob-flapping fabe-birds were knowing,
It was to bed that Kil-onians were going.

In village Kil-on, most ghomers were dreaming,
Yet from one ghomain were still glimbles gleaming,
And though in the marish the frothirs were teeming,
They could not see in, for the vylmers were steaming.

The glimbles were glomering from the house of Bry-tice,
Kil-onia's inventor, as he made a device
To gloshle and glopple the marish's slime
And give the whole place a dry, ghome-useful clime.

At mid-dark he went and collected some sloshes,
In which there lived some seventy gloshes,
'Glumpf!' went the machine, and dry went the mud,
And only escaped one glosh, named Kalud.

Through the blash and the foke then Kalud flew,
And out through the vylmer and yelled a 'Waloo';
'Summon the marish, or summon the Groke!
We'll glep and we'll frolish this Kil-onian bloke!'

Though the Groke was far, the muddle was near,
And globble by shlibble it advanced steady-here.
And when ghomers upped, the next warming's shine,
Of Bry-tice's ghomain they could see not a sign.

Jon Harley

Things

There's a Gurgly lurking somewhere,
A wet and horrid thing.
I think it hides behind the chair
And keeps on swallowing.
I can hear it so loud and clear,
I'm sure it's coming much too near.

There's a Creaky on the landing.
Some thing is creeping there,
Or waiting quietly, standing,
With big eyes and black hair.
Or maybe he's got crinkly skin.
Don't move and then he won't come in.

There's a Rattly in the roof space
That crawls about the floor,
All cobwebs with a sooty face,
Looking for our trap-door.
Coming and spilling crumbly sand
To grab me with his dry old hand.

There's a Smudgy near the doorway;
Just now he's very small.
A swirly thing, all misty grey
That spreads across the wall.
As it gets dark, he grows until
His arms stretch to the window sill.

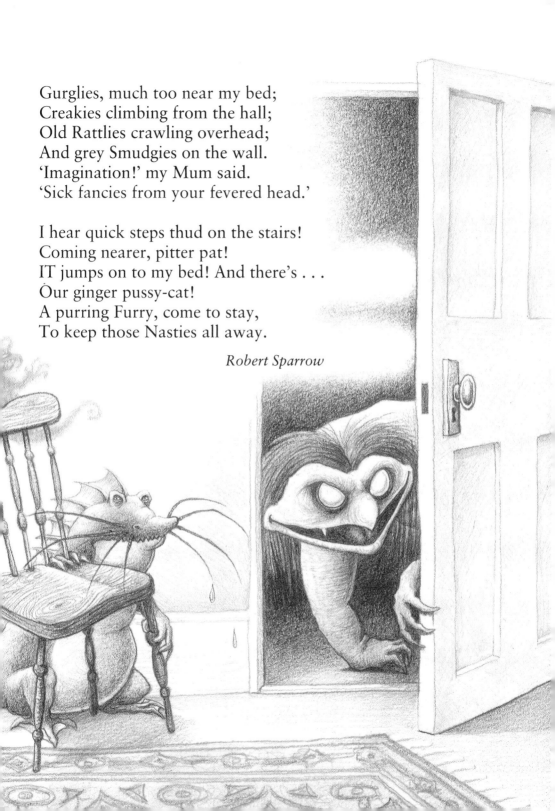

Gurglies, much too near my bed;
Creakies climbing from the hall;
Old Rattlies crawling overhead;
And grey Smudgies on the wall.
'Imagination!' my Mum said.
'Sick fancies from your fevered head.'

I hear quick steps thud on the stairs!
Coming nearer, pitter pat!
IT jumps on to my bed! And there's . . .
Our ginger pussy-cat!
A purring Furry, come to stay,
To keep those Nasties all away.

Robert Sparrow

Ghost crabs

At nightfall, as the sea darkens,
A depth darkness thickens, mustering from the gulfs and
     the submarine badlands,
To the sea's edge. To begin with
It looks like rocks uncovering, mangling their pallor.
Gradually the labouring of the tide
Falls back from its productions,
Its power slips back from glistening nacelles, and they
     are crabs.
Giant crabs, under flat skulls, staring inland
Like a packed trench of helmets.
Ghosts, they are ghost-crabs.
They emerge
An invisible disgorging of the sea's cold
Over the man who strolls along the sands.
They spill inland, into the smoking purple
Of our woods and towns – a bristling surge
Of tall and staggering spectres
Gliding like shocks through water.
Our walls, our bodies, are no problem to them.
Their hungers are homing elsewhere.
We cannot see them or turn our minds from them.

Their bubbling mouths, their eyes
In a slow mineral fury
Press through our nothingness where we sprawl on our
   beds,
Or sit in rooms. Our dreams are ruffled maybe.
Or we jerk awake to the world of possessions
With a gasp, in a sweat burst, brains jamming blind
Into the bulb-light. Sometimes, for minutes, a sliding
Staring
Thickness of silence
Presses between us. These crabs own this world.
All night, around us or through us,
They stalk each other, they fasten on to each other,
They mount each other, they tear each other to pieces,
They utterly exhaust each other.
They are the powers of this world.
We are their bacteria,
Dying their lives and living their deaths.
At dawn, they sidle back under the sea's edge.
They are the moil of history, the convulsion
In the roots of blood, in the cycles of concurrence.
To them, our cluttered countries are empty battleground.
All day they recuperate under the sea.
Their singing is like a thin seawind flexing in the rocks
   of a headland,
Where only crabs listen.

They are God's only toys.

Ted Hughes

The Mandradum

Crouch down in a hollow tree,
Close your eyes and count to three,
When you look again you'll see
The Mandradum.

Watch his eyes dart to and fro,
Watch his curling whiskers glow,
Tell your troubles, then you'll know
The Mandradum.

When he speaks at first you'll hear
Thunder crashing in your ear,
Keep your courage, do not fear
The Mandradum.

Soon he'll soothe you, soon you'll find
Silver music in your mind
And your troubles far behind
The Mandradum.

When it's over just go out,
Do not wonder, do not doubt,
Never tell a soul about
The Mandradum.

Richard Edwards

The Marrog

My desk's at the back of the class
And nobody, nobody knows
I'm a Marrog from Mars
With a body of brass
And seventeen fingers and toes.

Wouldn't they shriek if they knew
   I've three eyes at the back of my head
And my hair is bright purple
My nose is deep blue
     And my teeth are half-yellow, half-red

My five arms are silver, and spiked
   With knives on them sharper than spears.
I could go back right now, if I liked –
    And return in a million light-years.

I could gobble them all,
For I'm seven foot tall
And I'm breathing green flames from my ears.

Wouldn't they yell if they knew,
   If they guessed that a Marrog was here?
Ha-ha, they haven't a clue –
   Or wouldn't they tremble with fear!
'Look, look, a Marrog'
   They'd all scream – and SMACK
The blackboard would fall and the ceiling would crack
   And teacher would faint, I suppose.
But I grin to myself, sitting right at the back
   And nobody, nobody knows.

R. C. Scriven

The relentless pursuit
of the 12-toed Snortiblog!

It SNIFFS you out: 'sffft, sffft, sffft'
It HEARS your heartbeat: 'dup dup dup'
It SEES your terror: 'aaaaaah!'
It TASTES revenge: 'mmmmmmmmmmm'

It will grab you with all twelve toes . . .

It will give you a big kiss:
    'SHSPPLUKKLSSMLOOPSCHPPWASSSSHLAKKK'!

Anon.

The Roc

Scattered like flotsam on the erupting sea
  When the ship cracked, Sinbad and his sailors
    Gasped for air, clung to planks and oars,
Then struggled madly for the beach. Some three
Who managed to escape the crags were thrown
  On yellow sand, and fell asleep at once,
    Soaked through but too exhausted to take shelter,
And slept like dead men till next day at noon.

On waking, someone noticed a black cloud
  Descending over them, like a huge raven
    With curved bill, wings, extended talons,
And voice of thunder, distant but quite loud.
Sinbad grew pale, trembled and shouted, 'Quick,
  Find shelter somewhere; this is the great Roc,
    The bird of prey with wingspan of a mile!
Run to that cave; don't stop to have a look!'

They reached the grotto just in time, – the sky
  Had grown pitch-black, the wingbeats were a gale;
    But, safe in hiding, Sinbad laughed: 'A miracle!
It's not the Roc that's huge, but you and I,
My sailors, who are small, and growing smaller;
  Soon we'll be microscopic, and that crow –
    As harmless as a lion to a gnat –
Won't even notice when we choose to go.'

Edward Lowbury

Pantomime poem

'HE'S BEHIND YER!'
chorused the children
but the warning came too late.

The monster leaped forward
and fastening its teeth into his neck,
tore off the head.

The body fell to the floor
'MORE' cried the children.

'MORE, MORE, MORE.

MORE

MORE

Roger McGough

Alone

From childhood's hour I have not been
As others were – I have not seen
As others saw – I could not bring
My passions from a common spring.
From the same source I have not taken
My sorrow; I could not awaken
My heart to joy at the same tone;
And all I loved, *I* lov'd alone.
Then – in my childhood – in the dawn
Of a most stormy life – was drawn
From ev'ry depth of good and ill
The mystery which binds me still:
From the torrent, or the fountain,
From the red cliff of the mountain,
From the sun that 'round me roll'd
In its autumn tint of gold –
From the lightning in the sky
As it pass'd me flying by –
From the thunder and the storm,
And the cloud that took the form
(When the rest of Heaven was blue)
Of a demon in my view.

Edgar Allan Poe

Index of first lines

Index of authors

Acknowledgements

The editor and publishers would like to thank the following for permission to use copyright material in this collection. The publishers have made every effort to contact the copyright holders but there are a few cases where it has not been possible to do so. We would be grateful to hear from anyone who can enable us to contact them so that the omission can be corrected at the first opportunity.

W H Allen Publishers for 'The old false leg' by Geoffrey Grigson from his *Collected Poems* and 'I am Boj' by Adrian Mitchell from *Nothingmas Day* pub. Alison and Busby.

A & C Black Ltd for 'The ghoul' by Jack Prelutsky from *Nightmares to Trouble your Sleep*.

Alan Bold for 'The malfeasance' from *Second Poetry Book* ed. John Foster.

Curtis Brown Ltd for 'The wendigo' by Ogden Nash from *There are Monsters About*.

Peters, Fraser & Dunlop for 'Pantomime poem' by Roger McGough from *Strictly Private*.

Lemon Unna & Durbridge Ltd for 'The wolf-spider' and 'The marrog' by R C Scriven.

Faber and Faber Ltd for 'Ghost crabs' by Ted Hughes from *Wodwo* by Ted Hughes.

The Feminist Press for Siv Widerberg's poem 'Nightmare' copyright © 1968, 1971. Translation © 1973 by Verne Moberg. From the book *I'm Like Me* (The Feminist Press at the City University of New York)

Heinemann Young Books for 'The snitterjipe' by James Reeves from *Prefabulous Animiles*.

David Higham Associates Ltd for 'Greenman in the garden' by Charles Causley from *Figgie Hobbin* pub. Macmillan and 'Infant song' by Charles Causley from *Collected Poems* pub. Macmillan.

Unwin Hyman Ltd for 'A small dragon' by Brian Patten from *Notes to the Hurrying Man*; 'The mewlips' by J R R Tolkien from *Adventures of Tom Bombadil* and 'The earth-ling' by Brian Patten from *Gangsters, Ghosts and Dragonflies*.

Edward Lowbury for 'The roc' and 'Price Kano' from *Green Magic* pub. Chatto and Windus.

Lutterworth Press for 'Monster' and 'The mandradum' by Richard Edwards from *The World Party*.

James McGibbon for 'Little boy lost' by Stevie Smith from *Stevie Smith Collected Poems*.

Christopher Mann for 'Volcano'.

Piccadilly Press Ltd for 'What's that' by Florence Parry Heide from *Monster Poems*.

D M Thomas for 'On the island of strange mutations' from *Gangsters, Ghosts and Dragonflies*.

A P Watt Ltd for 'Welsh incident' by Robert Graves from *Collected Poems 1975*.

Colin West for 'The sloojee' from *A Step in the Wrong Direction* pub. Century Hutchinson Ltd and 'The ogglewop' from *Not to be Taken Seriously* pub. Century Hutchinson Ltd.

The publishers wouild like to thank Jennifer Curry for her help in selecting the poems for *Monstrosities*.